To:

_____

From:

_____

Date:

_____

HOME
IS RIGHT WHERE
YOU ARE

INSPIRED BY PSALM 23

WRITTEN AND ILLUSTRATED BY

RUTH CHOU SIMONS

Tommy
NELSON®

An Imprint of Thomas Nelson

Published in Nashville, Tennessee, by Tommy Nelson. Tommy Nelson is an imprint of Thomas Nelson. Thomas Nelson is a registered trademark of HarperCollins Christian Publishing, Inc.

Author is represented by Jenni Burke of Illuminate Literary Agency, www.illuminateliterary.com.

Tommy Nelson titles may be purchased in bulk for educational, business, fund-raising, or sales promotional use. For information, please email SpecialMarkets@ThomasNelson.com.

Scripture quotations are taken from the ESV® Bible (The Holy Bible, English Standard Version®). Copyright © 2001 by Crossway, a publishing ministry of Good News Publishers. Used by permission. All rights reserved. Minor typographical and punctuational changes were made for aesthetic purposes only.

ISBN 978-1-4002-4440-9 (eBook)
ISBN 978-1-4002-4439-3 (HC)

Library of Congress Cataloging-in-Publication Data is on file.

Written and illustrated by Ruth Chou Simons
Interior design by Kristen Sasamoto

Printed in Malaysia

24 25 26 27 28 VPM 6 5 4 3 2 1

Mfr: VPM / Rawang, Malaysia / August 2024 / PO #12179994

To my sons—
Caleb, Liam, Judah, Stone, Asa, and Haddon.

You were made to fly, but you'll never be far from home.

A Word from the Author

I am a mama to six boys (some of whom I've launched into the adult world!), and I wrote this book to articulate what I want them to remember as they begin their adult lives: that the love and faithfulness of God is incomparable.

The relationship between parents and children is the *most* rewarding and the *most* gut-wrenching: holding on tightly just to let them go; teaching them what we know and praying it sticks; running ahead of them until they're suddenly running ahead of us, ready to take flight. All the while, we're sowing the truth of God's Word and character, praying that the seeds we've sown take root and flourish.

Psalm 23 is one of those seeds. It speaks of God's love and faithfulness with beautiful pictures about what it means to be a sheep in the care of a good Shepherd. It reminds us that God is our dwelling place—our only *true* home. Psalm 23 is the song of one who has traveled with God and knows—without a shadow of a doubt—that He provides, comforts, shelters, and leads His people through every beautiful and hard place of life's journey. What more could a parent wish for their child than to sing that song?

Whether you read this book as a parent releasing your beloved children into adulthood or helping your little ones navigate the journey of life, my prayer is that *Home Is Right Where You Are* serves as a tether to the faithfulness of God. Because no twist or turn in your journey—no mountain or valley, no joy or grief—will find you alone when you walk with God.

Because of grace,

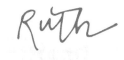

Listen close,
my sweet child,

To this one thing I know.
Let's walk together—
Hold my hand as we go.

The Lord is your keeper,
So all you need is yours—
Like the peace that He offers
And the rest He secures.

He knows the way to all that is true.

He's forever your home—
And always with you.

When you feel empty inside
Or there's an ache in your soul,
The Lord draws you close
And makes your heart whole.

Sometimes you'll journey
On paths so unclear.

You'll think you're TOO SMALL
And tremble with fear.

Look up, my darling,

In the dark of the night.
The Lord guides your steps—
And keeps you in sight.

Some days will be hard. You'll be troubled and blue

When others don't recognize

God's wonder in you.

But God **fills your cup**
With His comfort and care.

Hope, joy, and peace
Will spill out everywhere!

JOY

HOPE

PEACE

Child, never forget
Your Redeemer and Friend.
He's all that you need,

And **His**
love

has no end.

Someday your journey
May mean we're apart.

You'll fly from this nest
Here next to my heart.

God's
goodness
and mercy
will follow you there.

You'll never outrun

His grace and His care.

Wherever you go,
And whatever you do,

Here is a truth
I can promise to you:

No matter what, darling,
This one thing I know—

The Lord is your keeper
Wherever you go.

So follow Him bravely
For all of your days.
He keeps you close—
You won't lose your way.

You'll always be near me
When miles take you far.

For when **God** is with you . . .

home

is right where you are.

The Lord is my shepherd

I shall not want.
He makes me lie down in green pastures.
He leads me beside still waters.
He restores my soul.
He leads me in paths of righteousness
for his name's sake.
Even though I walk through the valley
of the shadow of death,
I will fear no evil,
for you are with me;
your rod and your staff,
they comfort me.
You prepare a table before me
in the presence of my enemies;
you anoint my head with oil;
my cup overflows.
Surely goodness and mercy shall follow me
all the days of my life,
and I shall dwell in the house of the Lord
forever.

Psalm 23